This edition published by Parragon Books Ltd in 2014 and distributed by

Parragon Inc.
440 Park Avenue South, 13th Floor
New York, NY 10016
www.parragon.com

Written by Kirsten Larsen
Illustrated by Ron Zalme

Printed in China

It's Sharing Day!

Bath · New York · Cologne · Melbourne · Delhi
Hong Kong · Shenzhen · Singapore · Amsterdam

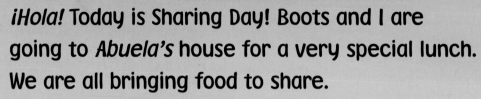

¡Hola! Today is Sharing Day! Boots and I are going to *Abuela's* house for a very special lunch. We are all bringing food to share.

Abuela is making *empanadas.* Boots is bringing a bunch of bananas. For dessert I am bringing rice and milk so we can make *arroz con leche.*

Map says we need to go to Benny's Barn
to get the milk. Then we need to go to the
Rice Fields to get some rice.
    Let's hurry so we can get to *Abuela's*
in time for lunch. Come on! *¡Vámonos!*

Look, there's Benny in his go-cart.

Hola, Benny! Boots and I were coming to see you.
We need some milk from you. Will you give us a ride
to the Barn so we can get some milk?

Benny said he'll share his go-cart with us and
give us a ride to the Barn. Hop on! *Gracias,* Benny!

We made it to Benny's Barn, and there's his grandma. *¡Hola!* We need to borrow some milk so we can make *arroz con leche* for our Sharing Day lunch. Will you share some milk with us? You will? *¡Gracias!*

Since Benny and his grandma shared with
us, let's invite them to our Sharing Day lunch.
They said they would bring some cowboy
cookies to share. *¡Delicioso!*

Where do we need to go now? We have to go to the Rice Fields to get some rice. We can take a shortcut through Isa's Flowery Garden. *¡Vámonos!* Let's go!

There are so many plants and flowers in Isa's Flowery Garden. Some of the flowers are so tall that we can't see over them. How will we know which way to go?

Isa is singing a special flower song for us, to show us which way to go! Now we can follow the path! *Gracias,* Isa!

Isa shared her flower song to help us find
our way through her Flowery Garden. Since Isa
shared something with us, let's invite her to our
Sharing Day lunch, too!

Isa will bring a fresh vegetable salad to share. Yum!

Uh-oh. It's almost lunchtime, and we still need to go to the Rice Fields to get some rice for our dessert. How can we get there quickly? Look, there's Tico in his plane. Let's ask Tico if he can help.

Tico is going to share his plane and give us a ride
to the Rice Fields. *Gracias,* Tico. *¡Vámonos!*

We made it to the Rice Fields. To get the rice,
we have to shake the rice plants. Will you count
the rice plants you see?

¡Uno, dos, tres, cuatro, cinco! Five rice plants!

Good job! Now we have enough rice to make *arroz con leche* for everyone.

Now let's go to *Abuela's* house for lunch. Since Tico shared his plane with us, let's invite him to come along. He's bringing yummy nut bread to share. *¡Muy bien!*

Yay! We made it to *Abuela's* house. Now *Abuela* has the milk and rice for our *arroz con leche*. She is making it right now.

Mmm. It smells yummy. I can't wait to eat!

Lunchtime! Look at all of this delicious food we can share. We have *empanadas,* bananas, cowboy cookies, vegetable salad, nut bread, and *arroz con leche* for dessert!

¡Vamos a comer! Let's go eat!

What a great Sharing Day! Benny shared his go-cart, Isa shared her song, Tico shared his plane, and everyone brought food to share for lunch.

What did you share today?

Share with Dora

Dora has a beautiful charm necklace that she wants to share with you! Put on the necklace and then color this picture of the very same charm. *¡Muy bonito!*

Now you be the designer! Create your very own heart necklace on this picture. *¡Fantástico!*

Who Shared What?

Dora's friends all shared something on Sharing Day. Work out what they each shared by tracing over the letters.

Benny shared his

 go-cart

Isa shared her

 song

Tico shared his

 plane

Everyone shared their

 food

Balloons for Everyone!

Dora has a balloon to share with each of her friends.
Which color balloon does each friend get?
Follow the paths to find out!

Boots   Benny   Tico   Isa

Sharing is Caring

Dora has made some lemonade and she wants
to share a glass with her best friend, Boots!
Add some color to the picture.

A Song to Share

Dora and Boots are sharing a song with the Fiesta Trio! Can you match the missing puzzle pieces to the spaces?

Thanks for your help! Goodbye! ¡Adiós!